DISNEP'S

The HAUNTED MANSION

WALT DISNEY PICTURES PRESENTS EDDIE MURPHY "THE HAUNTED MANSION" A ROB MINKOFF FILM TERENCE STAMP WALLACE SHAWN MARSHA THOMASON JENNIFER TILLY
MUSIC BY MARK MANCINA COSTUME DESIGNER MONA MAY SPECIAL MAKE-UP EFFECTS BY RICK BAKER VISUAL EFFECTS BY SONYPICTURES IMAGEWORKS, INC. EDITOR PRISCILLA NEDD FRIENDLY, A.C.E.
PRODUCTION DESIGNER JOHN MYHRE DIRECTOR OF PHOTOGRAPHY REMI ADEFARASIN, B.S.C. EXECUTIVE PRODUCERS BARRY BERNARDI ROB MINKOFF PRODUCED BY DON HAHN ANDREW GUNN
BASED ON WALT DISNEY'S HAUNTED MANSION WRITTEN BY DAVID BERENBAUM DIRECTED BY ROB MINKOFF Walt Disney Pictures
haunted-mansion.com

SCHOLASTIC

Scholastic Children's Books
Commonwealth House, 1-19 New Oxford Street
London WC1A 1NU, UK
a division of Scholastic Ltd
London ~ New York ~ Toronto ~ Sydney ~ Auckland
Mexico City ~ New Delhi ~ Hong Kong

First published in the USA by Random House Children's Books, a division
of Random House, Inc., New York, and simultaneously in Canada by
Random House of Canada Limited, Toronto, in conjunction with
Disney Enterprises, Inc., 2003
First published in paperback in the UK by Scholastic Ltd, 2004

ISBN 0 439 96303 6

Printed and bound by Nørhaven Paperback, Denmark

2 4 6 8 10 9 7 5 3 1

The Junior Novelization

Adapted by James Thomas

Based on the screenplay by
David Berenbaum

Based on Walt Disney's
Haunted Mansion

Produced by
Don Hahn and Andrew Gunn

Directed by Rob Minkoff

Still photography by Bruce McBroom

Prologue

Alone in her room, a lady dipped a quill pen into an inkwell. She was writing a letter. In the flickering candlelight, she wrote the final words, "My Love" and "For All Eternity". At the bottom she signed it "Elizabeth".

Carefully, she folded the letter and slipped it into a red envelope. She sealed the envelope with hot wax, stamping it with her personal insignia. The lady tucked the letter into her sleeve and picked up the mask resting on the corner of her desk. It was time to go to the masquerade.

A full moon hung low over the Gracey Manor, making the large house look magical. The road to the house was lined with ancient oak trees. Beneath the oaks, orange lanterns lit the way, guiding the Graceys' guests to the party. Carriage after carriage drove up the road and stopped in front of the house. Masked footmen stepped forwards to help the elegantly dressed guests out of their carriages.

The lady stepped from her carriage with her hood drawn over her face. In one hand she held the red letter. She walked into the grand hallway, following the sounds of music. Ornate statues, richly coloured paintings and grand antiques lined the hall. Alone, the lady glided past the other masked guests. Ahead lay a long, columned armoury and, past that, the ballroom. There, couples spun to a waltz being played by a small orchestra in one corner of the room.

At the entrance to the room, a footman held a silver tray. On the tray was a stack of invitations, all white. The lady stepped forwards and placed the red envelope on the stack. Through his mask, the footman stared nervously at the lady. She nodded at him, then slipped discreetly through the crowd.

The lady entered the library, leaving the noise of the ballroom behind. On the walls around her were portraits of nobles and aristocrats. They seemed to glare at her as she prepared to wait.

A short time later, a butler dressed in black exited the library and closed the door quietly behind him. He was the only person in attendance not wearing a mask. He approached the footman, took the stack of invitations in one hand and slipped the red envelope into his pocket.

The butler delivered the red letter to a man in another room of the mansion. The man wore a porcelain mask and a black cloak. He stood by a fireplace and read the letter. As he read, the man began to shake. The letter fluttered from his hands as he rushed out of the room.

In the grand hallway a grandfather clock began to chime the hour. The man ran through the house, racing against the chiming of the clock. Finally he burst into the library, but it was too late. The lady lay motionless on the floor, a goblet of poisoned wine in her hand.

The man fell to his knees and gathered the woman into his arms. Masked guests peered through the library doors as the man raised his head and screamed.

The Gracey family and their mansion soon fell into ruin. More than one hundred years passed as the dark and deserted Gracey Manor slumbered on its hill, waiting. . . .

Chapter 1

No one in Jim Evers' car was happy.

Jim owned a real estate business with his wife, Sara. His determination to be the most successful real estate salesman in New Orleans kept him out late almost every night showing houses to clients. The night before, he had been hours late for his wedding anniversary dinner. Now Sara was upset, and Jim felt terrible. In an attempt to make it up to her, he had loaded the whole family into his prized German luxury car to go for a weekend at the lake – after he and Sara had met with their new client.

In general, Sara felt that Jim spent too much time on the business, often neglecting their family. His late arrival to their anniversary dinner was just another disappointment in what had become a long line of disappointments. Then their new client had called and specifically requested that she meet him – without Jim. When Jim had learned about the client, he had insisted on coming along. Sara had wanted to postpone the meeting so that she could spend time with Jim and the kids, but Jim was never one to let a business opportunity pass him by.

The Everses' thirteen-year-old daughter, Megan, wasn't happy about things in general.

"This is so completely unconstitutional!" Megan complained to her dad from the backseat. "Why do I have to suffer?" Megan, who wanted to be at her friend Lori's house, groaned, "Mom, do I really have to be here?"

"I am not going to send you to an unchaperoned party with boys," said Sara sternly. Jim nodded in agreement.

Megan continued to groan, grimace and complain at low volume from the backseat. Jim gave her a look in the rear-view mirror.

He noticed Michael, his ten-year-old son, chewing.

"No snacking on expensive German leather!" Jim scolded. "The Germans hate crumbs. They will come over from Germany and get you!"

Michael sighed and put his food away.

The atmosphere in the car remained tense as they cruised down a narrow country lane. The road was surrounded by thick forest. The late-day sky slowly turned grey as a storm approached. Thunder rumbled menacingly.

The sky grew darker and lightning flashed. Jim turned on the headlights and was startled to see how close the forest was to the road. And the road had changed from pavement to dirt.

"Are we there yet?" Michael asked.

"There it is!" Sara said.

A large iron gate came into view. Jim pulled up to it and stopped. The gate swayed and squealed in the blowing wind. On each side of the gate stood a tall stone wall.

"Wow," said Jim, awed. "Now that's what I call a whole lotta gate. They must have like a possum problem around here or something."

"Really big possum," Michael said fearfully.

Jim honked the horn, then leaned his head out of his window. "Hello!" he called. "We're here! Hello!"

Jim leaned on the horn for a moment. When he stopped, they all listened. All they could hear was the wind whistling through the trees, the squeak of the rusty gate and the rumble of the approaching thunder.

Jim sighed and threw the car into park. He hopped out and tiptoed to the gate, trying his best to keep his expensive shoes clean.

"I gotta nick up my new shoes," he muttered.

He poked around in the shrubbery where the gate met the wall, looking for an intercom. "Hello!" he called. "Hello! Evers Real Estate!"

Out of sheer frustration, he started pressing everything on the gate that might be a call button. Sara got out of the car and walked along the wall. Suddenly, she gasped and pointed to a dark Victorian mansion sitting on a hill in the distance.

Jim followed the direction of her finger.

"Don't you just love these old houses?" Sara said with an awed sigh.

Jim didn't answer but went back to trying to open the locked gate. Even from this distance, the old mansion looked impressive. He did not want to let the opportunity to sell this house slip through his fingers.

"It's getting late," Sara said.

"This is not a problem," Jim replied, not making any real progress with the gate. Suddenly, the padlock popped open, and the heavy chain rattled to the ground. The rusted hinges squealed as the gate slowly swung open on its own.

Sara's mouth hung open in disbelief, and Jim stared wide-eyed. Then he said, "See. No problem."

He nodded as if the now open gate was all his doing and added, "Kind of creaky. That's going to need some lube."

Chapter 2

"Look at the architecture," Sara said as Jim drove the car towards the house. "This place is incredible."

"I was just thinking the same thing," Jim said gleefully, dollar signs dancing in his head.

"It gives me the creeps," grumbled Megan.

Michael scrunched down deeper into the back-seat, hugging his backpack closer for protection. The ancient, gnarled trees bent over the road, their moss-covered branches seeming to reach down, grasping for the car. The decaying house in the distance seemed just as eager as the trees for them to arrive. Its darkened windows were like the slick, black eyes of a spider waiting

for a fly to stumble into its web. Spiders
Michael's number one fear, but the weird
mansion was now running a close second.

Michael gulped and looked away from the
house. He stared at his sister and said, "I was just
thinking the same thing."

Chapter 3

"Bob Vila would have a field day with this place!" Jim chirped merrily as he stopped the car.

The house had been beautiful in its day, but now it was weathered and falling apart. Four huge ivory columns framed the double-fronted doors. Above the doors the house rose three storeys. It loomed over them, dark and shadowy.

Jim, Sara and Megan got out of the car. Megan slammed her door.

"Can you please not slam the door?" Jim barked.

"It's just a car, Dad," she protested.

Jim leaned down lovingly against his prized possession. "It's okay," he crooned, gently patting the car's hood. "She didn't mean it."

Sara and Megan rolled their eyes.

"Michael, come on," Jim said. "Let's go!"

Reluctantly, Michael climbed out of the car, clutching his backpack. Michael always had his pack ready – portable radio, first aid kit, and even his old baseball, just in case his dad ever had time to play catch with him. Having it handy gave him a sense of security.

"I want pizza," Michael said. "Hey, Dad, when we get to the lake, can we go to that pizza place where I ate the whole pie?"

Jim ignored his son's not-so-subtle hint to hurry so they could leave. As he walked round the side of the house, Michael followed him. Megan and Sara stared up at the mansion's impressive facade.

Thunder rumbled again, closer now. The wind was blowing hard. Leaves from the oak trees beside the house swirled around Jim and Michael.

Jim stopped dead in his tracks, staring at the grounds behind the house.

"Huh," he said. "Well, now, *that's* not

something you see every day."

In front of them sprawled an old graveyard. Megan and Sara had followed Michael and Jim round the side of the house. Now they stood next to Jim and stared.

Megan struggled to speak. "Oh . . . my . . . god!" she said. "Dead people!"

"They've got *dead people* in their backyard," Sara said, looking over the hundreds of gravestones that stretched into the gathering darkness behind the house. Her initial enthusiasm for the mansion began to wane.

"Okay. So?" said Jim, trying to come to grips with what he was seeing. "Some people have pools."

Megan was appalled. Her father just did *not* understand.

The darkness lifted momentarily as lightning flashed in the sky. Then rain started to fall.

Jim freaked. "Oh, no!" he said. "My suit! This is my good suit!"

Lifting his arms over his head in an effort to protect his clothes from the rain, Jim hurried back round the corner of the house.

Sara and the kids followed Jim and ran onto the front porch. The wood was old and warped. It creaked as the family walked across to the two huge doors. Carved into each of the doors was a lion's head surrounded by snakes.

Jim knocked, and the sound echoed and boomed inside the house. Michael and Sara glanced at each other.

"Hello. Anybody? Evers Real Estate!" Jim called. "Hello! Hello! Real estate man!"

Jim waited a moment, then cautiously pressed against one of the doors. With a creak, it swung open. Jim walked inside, with Sara right behind him. Megan put her arm around Michael as they stepped through the door.

On the other side they found a grand hallway, two storeys high. Candles burned dimly along the rich wooden walls. The floor was covered in thick dark rugs and the windows were hung with heavy velvet curtains. Carved doors and archways led to corridors in every direction. A grand staircase rose at the end of the hall.

The Everses stood quietly for a minute,

stunned. Even Jim had to take it all in for a moment.

Sara stopped to inspect the carvings on the wall. Every detail was lavish but tasteful.

Michael was staring at an ivory sculpture, when a spider scurried across a cobweb. He jumped back. "Mom, this place has bugs," he said.

Sara was examining a stone statue and barely listening. "Yes, Michael," she said distractedly. "I'm sure this place has lots of things."

She was about to check out the painting behind the statue when she thought she heard the ever-so-faint beating of a heart. She turned her head, trying to catch the sound, but just as quickly as it had come, it was gone.

Then, somewhere nearby, hinges creaked and a door slammed. Everyone held their breath. Someone was coming.

Chapter 4

"Sara Evers?"

They all turned as a tall, grey-haired man emerged from the deep shadows around one of the doors. He was dressed in the formal clothes of a butler; his face was pale and thin.

Before Sara could say a word, Jim stepped in front of her and extended his hand.

"Yes, that's us," Jim said, flashing the man a smile. "Jim Evers, Evers Real Estate, at your service."

The butler ignored Jim's hand and glanced around the room at the rest of the family.

"We're not expecting . . . others," he said.

"Yes, I'm sorry— " Sara began.

"Yes, but when we discovered the enormity . . . the complexity of handling this magnificent and unique estate," Jim interrupted, grinning at the stiff butler, "we were determined to provide you with every resource at the disposal of Evers and Evers."

Sara shook her head.

"Yes, sir," the butler finally said. "My name is Ramsley. We shall have to place other settings."

"Great!" Jim said. Then he looked confused. "Other settings for what?" he asked.

"Dinner, sir," said Ramsley as he led the family through a door into a long hall lined on both sides with suits of armour. "Master Gracey wishes to discuss his affairs over dinner."

"Bu—" Michael started to complain. He was still hoping to have a pizza dinner with his dad. Jim quickly covered Michael's mouth.

"I'm sorry. We have other plans," Sara said, wanting to remind her husband that they did, in fact, have plans to spend time together as a family.

Jim gave his family a come-on-it'll-be-fun look

as they followed Ramsley to the end of the hall, where huge double doors opened into an immense ballroom. In the middle of the room stood a long table covered with a white silk cloth. Two large candelabras glowed at each end. Across the room stood a grand pipe organ. A fire roared in a beautiful marble fireplace. Tall paned windows dominated another wall and let in the dim grey light of the storm.

At the table a maid and a footman were laying out more place settings. They turned and stared at the family. Then, given a stern look from Ramsley, they hurriedly finished their work and left the room.

"The master shall be with you shortly," Ramsley said. Then he bowed and followed the servants out of the room.

"Carry on," Jim said jauntily, pleased with the situation.

Sara was frowning at him. Jim ignored her look and turned to Michael. "Hey, Mikey, this isn't so bad. How would you like to eat like this at home?"

Michael slumped into one of the chairs at the table, clearly disappointed. Lightning flashed outside, and the lights flickered.

Sara was shaking her head at Jim when she caught sight of something behind him. She walked over to inspect the fireplace.

"Incredible," she breathed, utterly captivated.

The images were of angels caught in fire and brimstone. Sara ran her hand over the elaborate work.

"I've never seen anything like this," she said.

"You haven't?" asked a man's voice from behind them.

The Everses turned to find a man standing in the shadows by the windows, staring out at the rain.

"My grandfather spared no expense when he built this mansion," the man continued.

He turned, and the Everses saw that the man was in his early thirties. He was handsome, with dark hair and brooding eyes. His suit was expensive and impeccably tailored.

Jim rushed over. "Well, Grandpa had some

really good taste, there. Jim Evers," he added, introducing himself. "Evers Real Estate."

The man glanced nervously at Jim. He seemed strangely agitated. Finally, he said, "Edward. Edward Gracey."

He bowed slightly, then turned and stared at Sara.

"Yeah," said Jim. "And this is my wife, Sara."

Sara smiled. "Very nice to meet you, Mr Gracey."

Gracey kept staring at Sara as she introduced the children. "And this is Megan, and our son, Michael," she continued.

Gracey glanced at the children. Michael sidled behind Megan, avoiding Gracey's eyes.

"You have very beautiful children, Ms Evers," said Gracey finally.

"Well, you know, I kicked in some chromosomes, too," Jim jokingly butted in.

Behind them they heard Ramsley say, "Children. Madam."

They turned to find that Ramsley had pulled out two chairs for Sara and Megan.

"Oh, thank you, Mr Ramsley," Sara said, walking to the table. Everyone else followed her to their places.

As Sara took her seat, Ramsley said, "The master was so very pleased when he heard you could come on such short notice. We wouldn't have called you here so abruptly, but the master felt he had no other choice."

"Termites?" Jim asked.

Ramsley glanced at his master, who was fidgeting nervously at the head of the table. "No, sir. Lately there have been more . . . disturbances," Ramsley explained.

Thunder rolled above the house as Gracey stared at Jim. "I am afraid the house has a bit of— a bit of history to it," Gracey said.

"Oh, of course," Jim said, pretending to understand. "But the right agent can use that to add to the value."

Gracey's brow creased at Jim's remarks. Then the servants entered with the food, and everyone began eating. This gave Gracey a chance to speak to Sara. "What do you think of the house,

Ms Evers?"

Sara smiled warmly at him. "I think it's absolutely incredible, Mr Gracey."

"It's super-incredible!" Jim quickly put in.

"I mean, just the Italian influence . . ." Sara said, her eyes sparkling with enthusiasm as she looked around the room. Jim frowned as she spoke, frustrated that he wasn't the one doing the talking.

"The Renaissance style of this room," Sara continued. "The molding, the filigree – just the amazing attention to detail. It's stunning. It's just— it's just you never see houses like this, Mr Gracey. At least I don't. So for me, it's like walking into some kind of fairy tale."

Gracey smiled at Sara. He was impressed by her knowledge. "Yes, Ms Evers," he said. "Great care and love went into this house."

Gracey fell silent but continued to stare at Sara. He seemed transfixed. Thunder rumbled outside as Michael and Megan exchanged glances.

Jim was also aware of how intently Gracey

seemed to focus on his wife. He spoke up. "How's the plumbing?"

The lights flickered again, and a chill wind swept through the room. Michael shivered and glanced around nervously.

"Copper plumbing?" Jim rattled on.

Looking uncomfortable, Gracey got up from the table and walked to the window.

"This house," he said, ignoring Jim and staring out at the storm. "It haunts me."

Chapter 5

Outside, lightning cracked the dark sky as the storm grew even more intense. Rain lashed at the mansion, and the wind howled through the eaves.

In the hall outside the ballroom, the maid, the footman, and the cook huddled together, whispering. They quickly got back to work as Ramsley walked past them and back into the ballroom.

Gracey stood next to the fireplace and stared into the fire. "They usually come at night. Only at night."

Michael spoke up nervously, never taking his eyes off a candle sliding slowly across the table as if moved by an invisible hand. "What? What comes at night?"

Gracey looked up with a pained expression on his face. He turned to Jim and stared at him intensely. "Tell me, Mr Evers. Do you believe in ghosts?"

Michael's eyes grew wide. Megan glanced at him and gave him a this-guy's-a-loon look.

"Ghosts?" Jim said, thinking fast. "Sure, yeah, I believe in ghosts. Although we probably don't want to emphasize that. We're better off talking about how many bathrooms you have. People go crazy for bathrooms! So let's just stay off the whole ghost thing. At least, you know, for now."

Thunder crashed. Ramsley walked to the window and peered out. "The storm has swollen the river," he said.

"What's that?" Jim asked.

Ramsley turned. "The storm has flooded the roads. I'm afraid there'll be no leaving the mansion tonight."

"What?" Megan cried.

Gracey nodded and turned to his guests,

smiling warmly. "Of course, you are more than welcome to spend the night."

Sara glanced at Jim. "Oh, I really don't think we should."

Michael nodded in agreement.

"I am afraid there is no other way," Gracey said. "Ramsley will show you to your rooms."

Gracey then turned and left them with the butler.

Jim turned to smile at his very unhappy family and said, "He seems real nice."

Candelabra in hand, Ramsley led the Evers family up the front stairs. Dim lights lined the corridor. Outside, thunder rolled. Michael clung to Megan as they passed a huge, wall-sized painting of a horrific battle between heaven and hell.

"Oooh, that's a nice picture," Jim said, stopping to admire it.

"It's a painting of Armageddon, sir," said Ramsley. "The Day of Judgment. Where everyone is judged. Judged by the fires of hell. It has always watched over this house."

"Huh," Jim said thoughtfully.

As they continued down the corridor, Michael fearfully glanced back at the painting. The eyes in the painting seemed to be following him. He snapped his head in the other direction, only to see their reflections in a large mirror. Someone else seemed to be with them, but when he looked round, there were only his family and the butler. Michael shivered.

He hurried up next to Sara as Ramsley stopped in front of a door and took a key out of his pocket.

"I believe the children will be comfortable in this room," he said.

Ramsley unlocked the door and opened it. Inside was a large, shadow-filled bedroom decorated with heavy, dark furniture.

Megan glanced through the doorway. "Yeah, great," she said. "Looks really homey."

Sara smiled at her children reassuringly. "Go ahead. I'll come back."

Jim added in a whisper, "When you flush the

toilet, see how quickly it refills."

Megan slammed the door in Jim's face. Jim smiled at the door and then turned to Ramsley.

"Um," he said. "Great kids."

"I'm sure, sir," said Ramsley tonelessly.

Ramsley crossed the hall and unlocked another door. "I hope you and madam will find this room to your liking."

The door creaked open to reveal a grand bedroom decorated in the same style as Megan's and Michael's.

"Oh, this is great," said Jim. "Honey, it's like spending the night in a fine hotel."

"Will there be anything else you require, sir?" Ramsley asked.

"What about the chocolates?" Jim asked.

Ramsley raised an eyebrow. "Pardon?"

Jim decided to forget the joke. Ramsley stared at him humourlessly, then walked away.

Across the corridor, in the other room, Michael was sitting in bed with the covers up to his shoulders. Megan was stomping around the room, trying to get through to her friends on her mobile phone.

"This is a nightmare," Megan said. "I could've been at Lori's house. Instead I'm sleeping in this creepy bedroom with *you*."

Megan looked around with disgust at the dark, sombre room. She shook her head, then noticed that Michael was staring at their door.

"What is it?" she asked.

Michael nodded sadly at their door. "They're arguing again."

Megan listened. Michael was right. She could just hear their parents' raised voices through the door.

"Flirting? What are you talking about?" Sara asked exasperatedly.

"Your *boyfriend*, Fancy Pants," Jim said, and then mockingly added in an imitation of her voice, "Oh, Mr Gracey, it's like walking into a fairy tale."

"In the first place, we're not even supposed to be here," Sara responded angrily. "We're *supposed* to be at the lake!"

"What am I supposed to do? I can't control the weather," Jim shouted.

"That's not the point," Sara said, trying to calm herself. "You couldn't resist. You just had to come."

Jim also tried to be rational. "Yes, because this is a great opportunity for *us*."

"Not for *us*," she said, shaking her head. "For *you*. Work is the only thing you care about any more."

"Well, you like it fine when I bring you expensive gifts," he retaliated, pointing to the beautiful watch on her wrist and feeling hurt that she didn't consider the time and love he had put into picking it out for her as an anniversary gift. "I guess it's fine when I work hard for that."

Sara took off the watch and threw it down on the bed in disgust. She turned away, walked into the bathroom and closed the door.

Chapter 6

Jim stood alone in the middle of the room, crestfallen.

"Oh, jumpin' geez!" Jim exclaimed. Startled, he found Ramsley standing directly behind him.

"Pardon the intrusion, sir," Ramsley said, "but the master was wondering if he might have a word with you in the library."

Jim quickly collected himself. "Oh. A word? Oh, good." He straightened his tie. "Well, I'd like to have a word with him, too. Time to talk a little turkey."

"Yes, turkey," Ramsley said blandly. "Very good, sir. If you'll follow me."

Jim turned back to the bathroom door. "Hey,

Sara, I'll be right back. Okay?"

When there was no answer, Jim followed Ramsley into the hall and down the stairs.

"Hey, Ramses," Jim said, checking out the butler's pale skin. "I know this guy in the city with this really great tanning salon. I think you might really like it. . . ."

As the two men passed through the grand hallway, a grandfather clock chimed. Ramsley led Jim into the library. The sounds of wind and rain filled the dark-panelled room. Gas lamps along the walls shone dimly on case after case of leather-bound books.

". . . and that way you get a nice, smooth tan," Jim was continuing to explain. "I think it will really make a difference with the ladies."

"Yes," Ramsley said. "I'll look into it."

Ramsley led Jim through the library and into an eight-sided room that appeared to be a study. A dark wooden desk sat in the middle of the room. Books and paintings lined the walls. One large window looked out on the night and the ferocious storm.

"Would you care for a drink while you wait, sir?" Ramsley asked.

"Sure," Jim said. "Don't mind if I do."

While Ramsley poured Jim a drink at a small bar along one wall, Jim examined one of the larger paintings. It was a portrait of Gracey.

"You know what I was thinking?" Jim said. "I was thinking I really got to get me one of these. I think it would look really nice in my house. You know, just a big picture of me. Add a little touch of class. A little elegance."

Ramsley walked over with Jim's drink. "Yes. Very elegant, sir," he said, handing Jim the glass.

"Ooh, good, the fancy stuff," Jim said. "What is this? Like a margarita?"

"It is a specialty of the house, sir," Ramsley said dryly.

"Oh, yeah?" said Jim. "Well, *L'chaim.*"

Jim raised his glass in a toast, then drank it down. Ramsley moved to the window and closed the curtains.

"How long have you been butler?" Jim asked.

"A long time," Ramsley said. A thin smile of

icy amusement crossed his face, and he added, "Longer than you might expect."

"So tell me, Ramses," Jim said, putting his glass down on the desk. "This boss of yours. What's he into?"

Ramsley stared at Jim for a long moment, then said, "The master has a great appreciation for art, literature and beauty."

"And this ghost stuff," said Jim. "What's that?"

"You don't believe in ghosts, sir?" asked Ramsley.

Jim laughed. "Here's what I believe," he said. "You go around the track *once*. So run full out all the way."

Ramsley looked uncomfortable. He stared at Jim a moment, then said, "Mr Evers, can I confide in you?"

"Well, sure, buddy," Jim said, thinking he was really going to get the straight story now.

Ramsley looked down, and his shoulders slumped. "The master is not well," he said. "He has not been well for a long, long time. This house – it consumes him. He must leave this house, Mr Evers. He must move on. It is of the gravest importance, I assure you. Or I fear . . . the very worst."

"We're on the same page," Jim said. "Just let me sell this house for you. And you and your boss can move to Boca. How's that sound?"

Ramsley took a deep breath and suddenly straightened up. Smoothing his vest, he said curtly, "The master shall be with you shortly."

Then he bowed and left the room, closing the doors behind him. Jim wandered around the library, checking out the books. He was surprised to find that a lot of them were about the dark arts of black magic – voodoo, spells and witchcraft.

"Art and literature, huh," he said. "And voodoo. Dude's into voodoo."

Jim grabbed a book at random from a shelf and sat down in a large leather chair.

"Nice," he said. He opened the book and crossed his legs, accidentally knocking over a decanter of wine on a side table. It shattered, spilling its contents all over the floor.

Jim jumped up. "Oh, geez, now I've done it.

Now I've done it."

He pulled out his handkerchief and tried to mop up the mess he had made. He quickly realized one handkerchief was not going to be enough for the job. He called for Ramsley and got no response.

"Club soda will knock that right out," he said, grabbing the bottle of soda from the bar and dabbing it on his handkerchief.

As he bent over the spill, his behind bumped into a statue on the bookshelf, snapping its head back.

"Oh, great! Now I've busted the bust," Jim groaned. He did not see that the bookcase had slid open behind him, revealing a secret passageway.

Jim gingerly moved the statue's head back into place. As he moved it, the panel in the bookcase also slid back into place. He quickly realized that the head was on a hinge. He pushed the head back again. Once again, the panel opened, and this time Jim noticed it.

"Huh, a secret room," he grunted in surprise.

"Cool. I wonder where it goes?"

He stepped into the passageway. The panel slid closed and everything went black.

"Hey! Let me out!" Jim cried, beating on the back of the hard wooden panel. "Ramsley? Hey, somebody! Push the head. Push the head."

Nothing.

"Where's that freaky albino when you need him?" Jim asked no one in particular.

Jim searched through the darkness with his hands, hoping to find a lever or perhaps a seam between the panel and the wall that he could use to pry open the secret doorway.

"Just great. I'm trapped," he complained when he did not find anything. He reached into his pockets to see if he had a pack of matches. *Yes*, he thought as his fingers found the matchbox. He quickly pulled out a match and lit it. The only thing in sight was an ancient stone staircase leading up.

"Ow!" Jim cried as the match burned two of his fingers.

Standing alone in the darkness, licking his

fingers, Jim knew he had no choice. He lit another match and walked over to the staircase. He only had one way to go.

Up.

Chapter 7

Upstairs, Megan was pacing back and forth in her and Michael's room, trying to get through to her friends on her mobile phone.

"Still no reception," she said. "Unbelievable. It must be this stupid storm or something."

"Do you think it will stop soon?" Michael asked. He was in bed with the covers pulled up.

"How do I know?" Megan snapped.

Frustrated, Megan stalked into the bathroom, punching numbers into her mobile phone again. A moment after she left, the curtains around the window billowed out gently, as if pushed by a soft breeze. But the window was closed.

Michael looked around the room. A music

box he hadn't noticed before suddenly began to play. The chimes played an eerily haunting melody. The two mechanical figures dressed in masquerade costumes and masks began to spin in imitation of a dance.

A slow heartbeat sounded as a brilliant sparkle of white light formed just inside the window. It began to spin, growing into a ball of pulsating light. Then it floated across the room towards Michael.

Michael's eyes widened as he began to quiver with fear. He puckered his lips, trying to speak.

"Mmm-Mmm-Mmm-Megan!"

"What is it, a spider?" she asked, storming back into the room. She knew that of all Michael's fears, spiders were definitely the worst.

"It's a ghost ball," Michael said with uncharacteristic certainty. After all, what else could it be?

The small hairs on the back of Megan's neck began to rise. Out of the corner of her eye, she saw a soft glow over her shoulder. Without turning her head, she shifted her eyes and saw the ball of light hanging right next to her!

Megan dropped her phone and staggered to the bed. She and Michael watched the ball float to the centre of the room. It moved towards the door, then paused. After a moment, Megan got up and walked towards it. The ball floated closer to the door and waited again.

"Wow," said Megan. "I think— I think it wants us to follow it or something."

"What?" Michael gasped. "You're crazy."

The ball floated into the door – and disappeared. Then it popped back through the door and into the room.

"It does," Megan said. "It wants us to follow it."

Michael looked at Megan as if she'd lost her mind. The ball disappeared through the door again.

"Come on," Megan said, moving to the door.

Michael shook his head so hard that his glasses bounced back and forth on his nose.

"Fine," Megan said. She opened the door. "Then stay here. Alone."

She walked through the doorway and started down the hall after the ball of light. Michael glanced around the empty room. The shadows in the corners seemed to be growing.

Megan hadn't taken more than a few steps before Michael dashed out of their room and smacked into her.

"Ow!" Megan cried. "Watch it! Watch it!"

They were following the light down the corridor together when their parents' bedroom door opened.

Sara poked her head out and saw the kids in the corridor. "Megan!" she said.

The kids jumped. At the end of the corridor, the light zipped round the corner, out of sight.

"What are you two doing?" Sara asked.

Michael pointed down the corridor. "Mom, there's a ghost b—"

Megan elbowed him in the side, cutting him off. "We couldn't sleep," she said. "So we figured we'd take a walk."

"Take a walk?" Sara asked. "Well, I don't think that's a very good idea. This isn't your house, you know. Now go back to your room, and I'll see you in the morning."

"Okay, Mom," Megan said.

"But what about the—" Michael began.

Megan quickly covered her brother's mouth and hurried him back down the hall.

"Night, Mom," she said.

"Goodnight," said Sara.

Megan pushed Michael into their bedroom and slammed the door. Michael opened his mouth to say something, but Megan shushed him and put her ear to the door. Not hearing anything, she quietly opened it – to find Sara still standing there, her arms crossed. Megan quickly shut the door again.

Meanwhile, Jim had come to a passageway leading off into more darkness. He was down to his last match.

From farther down the passageway, a woman's voice echoed, "Serpents and spiders, tail of a rat . . . a rat. Call in the spirits wherever they're at."

All around him Jim heard ghostly moans and wails, and a fierce wind blew past him towards the woman's voice.

"Rap on a table; it's time to respond," came the woman's voice. "Send us a message from somewhere beyond."

In the distance Jim heard the sounds of unearthly drums and tambourines.

"Yeah, okay, I was supposed to meet with Mr Gracey," Jim called out. "But I got trapped in the wall, see, and . . ."

A green, ethereal light spilled out of an open door farther down the hall. Jim followed the light to the doorway and stepped into the room.

Jim couldn't believe his eyes. On a table in the middle of the room sat a crystal ball in an elaborate gold base. All around the room were unlit candles and tarot cards. The walls were heavily draped.

The door behind him slammed shut, and the candles burst into life. Jim had the eerie feeling that someone was watching him. A ghostly head began to form in the crystal ball. The head slowly turned so that it was facing him. It was green and seemed to be the head of a Gypsy woman. A dead Gypsy woman.

Her eyes snapped open, and the head spoke. "I am Madame Leota. Whom do you seek?"

Not wanting to believe the head was talking to him, Jim pointed to himself.

"Yes, you," said the head.

"This is crazy," Jim said, looking around to see who might be playing a joke on him. "I can hear you, but I can't see you."

"I am Madame Leota," said the head. "Seer of all. Voice to the spirits. Whom do you seek?"

"Seek?" Jim said. "I'm not seeking *nobody*!"

Magically a cushioned chair scooped up Jim and slid to a stop directly in front of the table.

"Let me outta here!" Jim said. A great wind rushed through the room. The candlelight flickered.

"Silence!" commanded Madame Leota. "Whom do you seek?"

"I'm seeking my car, okay?" said Jim. "And my keys and me driving outta here with my family."

"Then you must look within," said Madame Leota.

"Within?" Jim said. "I don't want to look within! I want to look without! Are you deaf?"

Madame Leota didn't answer. Seeking prophecy, she closed her eyes and concentrated. Shaking and quivering, her table slowly rose into the air.

"There is great evil in this house," she intoned. "A devil's curse! It seeks to destroy you!"

Jim's chair also began to rise off the floor. Suddenly, he was at eye level with Madame Leota again, and gripping the chair for dear life.

"What seeks to destroy me?" Jim asked. "I haven't done anything."

"Your family is at stake!" Leota continued. "Your very life is at stake! Break the curse! There is no escape for you unless you lift its spell!"

Jim stared at Leota. "Come again?" he asked.

A violent wind burst into the room as Leota repeated her words at a deafening volume. Jim squinted in pain. Out of the corner of his eye, he saw tortured spirits writhing in the demonic wind.

All around him the candles flickered low, and the room grew dark and quiet. Leota's closed eyes started to twitch.

"Lift us up to the light," she intoned. "Lead us through this stormy night."

Out of the darkness, more wispy white ghosts swirled. They flew about the room, moaning and wailing.

"Devils and demons, all stand before," called Madame Leota. "Break this curse, to find heaven's door! Evil and darkness have fallen this night. But now, to survive, you must regain lost sight."

"First, I must gain new underwear!" Jim joked, trying to stay calm.

Another sudden explosion of wind and light spun Jim's chair so that he hung upside down. He screamed in terror.

"There's no place like home," he whimpered. "There's no place like home. There's—"

Greenish vapour swirled around Leota. Her

eyes popped open and she began to talk rapidly.

"Go, Mr Evers. Save yourself!" she said. "Save your family! Release her! Release us all!"

Jim's chair whipped him wildly around the room, until his arms and legs were suddenly released and he was thrown to the ground.

In the passageway outside Madame Leota's room, everything was quiet. Then the door was flung open and Jim came running out, screaming at the top of his lungs!

Chapter 8

Sara made her way carefully down the stairs and into the house's grand hallway. It was completely dark except for the occasional flash of lightning coming through the windows.

She paused. A slow chill trickled down her spine. She had the definite sense that somebody – or something – was watching her.

Lightning flashed, and Ramsley stepped forwards. "Ms Evers, can I help you?" he asked.

Sara jumped. "Oh!" she gasped. "Yes, Ramsley, I was just looking for my husband."

"Ah, indeed. I left him in the library," Ramsley said. He motioned towards the back of the hall. "Right through those doors."

"Great," Sara said. "Thank you so much."

"Of course, madam," Ramsley said.

Sara walked to the library doors. Ramsley watched her go.

In the library, Sara looked around the room as she crossed to the shelves of books. She reached up and lightly touched the leather-bound volumes. Suddenly, she heard a noise across the room.

"Jim?" she asked. She walked to the other side of the room. There was a man sitting with his back to her.

"Jim, what in the world are you doing in here?" she asked. "What do you think—"

Sara stopped abruptly. It wasn't Jim sitting in the chair. It was Mr Gracey. He was staring into the fire.

"Oh, I'm sorry," Sara said. "I thought you were my husband."

Gracey looked up and stared into Sara's eyes. Feeling uncomfortable, Sara stepped back and knocked over a stack of books. She bent to pick them up.

"Here, let me get that," Gracey said, stooping to help her gather up the books. Sara was suddenly aware of how close they were to each other. The candlelight in the room swayed softly. The sound of the storm seemed suddenly distant.

Gracey gazed at Sara, looking almost longingly at her hair. Sara noticed, and Gracey quickly looked down again and concentrated on tidying the books.

"This house," Sara said. "It's been in your family for generations. It's your home. Why do you want to sell it?"

Gracey stared at her a moment. "I think for you to understand, I really must show you."

Sara stood, slightly alarmed.

"It's all right," Gracey said, also standing. "There's nothing to be afraid of."

He smiled, and Sara smiled back. Gracey gestured for her to precede him through the doorway. As soon as she'd passed, the smile dropped from Gracey's face, leaving only a troubled stare.

Meanwhile, Megan and Michael had left their room and managed to find the ball of glowing white light again. They'd followed it downstairs and into a maze of corridors.

"How are we supposed to get back to our room?" Michael asked. "We didn't leave bread crumbs or anything."

"Michael, we're not going back to our room," Megan said. "We're going somewhere."

"Well, I think the ball is lost, too," Michael said.

The ball came to a stop next to an antique lift with an iron grille for a door. As the kids watched, the grille creaked open.

"Come on," Megan said, stepping into the lift. "I told you it was leading us somewhere. Just relax. Everything's going to be fine. Everything's gonna be just—"

Megan broke off as she realized that her brother hadn't followed her. Michael was standing alone in the corridor.

"You don't know the last time that thing was inspected," Michael said, sounding strangely like his father.

"Where's your sense of adventure?" Megan asked.

"I left it back in the room," her brother replied, trying to think of a way out of this particular adventure. "Maybe I should go get it."

"Well?" Megan asked. "Are you coming or not?"

Michael fearfully inched around the ball of light and into the lift. The glowing ball floated into the lift with them.

"This is really against my better judgment," Michael muttered.

With a screech, the lift door closed. Michael looked at his sister as the lift began to slowly ascend. Upon reaching the attic, the cage door creaked open once more.

The ball of white light floated into the room. In its glow they could see a low-ceilinged space full of crates and boxes and bins. It looked like no one had been there for years.

"Come on," Megan said as the ball started floating across the room. The kids followed it past broken mirrors and glass bell jars. The light disappeared through an upside-down keyhole.

Megan cautiously looked through the keyhole. The light was shining brightly in a room filled with clothes, antiques, paintings and books. It was a room full of memories.

The doorknob began to rattle. Megan drew back as the door popped open. With a glance at each other, the kids stepped into the room.

"Wow," Megan said. "Would you look at all this stuff?" She began to sift through one of the boxes and discovered a dusty porcelain masquerade mask.

As Michael looked around, a painting caught his eye. It was a portrait of a woman in a seventeenth-century gown. He squinted at it through his large glasses.

Then his eyes grew wide. "Megan," he said.

"What?" Megan asked, examining the mask she'd found.

"Megan!" Michael repeated.

"What?" she asked. She looked up and saw the portrait. The ball of light floated over so that it glowed on the face of the person in the portrait. Megan gasped.

It was their mother!

Chapter 9

"Who goes there?" a voice called.

Michael hid behind a clothing mannequin as the ball of light disappeared. In the doorway, carrying a lantern, stood the male servant they had seen before, the footman. His name was Ezra.

"What are you doing here?" Ezra demanded. "You're not supposed to be up here!"

Ignoring him, Megan pointed to the painting. "Who is that?" she asked.

"Oh, that?" Ezra said, momentarily forgetting to be upset. "Yes. Why that's— none of your business! That's who! Now, be on your way!"

He started pushing the kids out. "Come on, it's way past your bedtime."

"Her name was Elizabeth," said a woman's voice. It was the maid, Emma.

"And who asked you?" Ezra said. "Did anyone ask you? Do you want to get us into more trouble?"

"How could we possibly get in more trouble?" Emma replied.

"I don't know!" said the footman. "And quite frankly, I don't want to find out!"

"Are you kids hungry?" Emma asked, changing the subject. "Does anyone want a cookie?"

"Cookies?" Ezra thundered. "Don't offer them cookies! They're trespassers! Trespassers don't get cookies! They shouldn't be up here! This is none of their concern!"

"Of course it's their concern," Emma said. "They're involved!"

"Involved in what?" Megan asked.

"Well, for starters . . ." Emma began. As the kids watched, she rose off the floor. She twirled in mid-air, bluish dust shimmering around her. The maid's skin changed to a ghostly white.

Ezra was beside himself. "What is she doing?"

he thundered. "Oh, now she's done it!"

Michael shivered in terror. "Gh-gh-gh—" he stammered.

Emma smiled at him. "Ghost," she said. "It's okay. You can say it."

"No. Really. I can't," Michael said matter-of-factly.

"Oh, now you have really done it!" Ezra said. "*He*'s not going to be happy about any of this! And I'm not gonna be the one who tells him! Do you understand the ramifications?"

The kids watched, stunned, as Ezra stormed right out of his skin and stalked over to Emma. "We have to stay in line!" he said.

"Oh, relax," Emma said. "We all want to break the curse!"

"Well, then, leave it up to the master and stay out of it!" Ezra said. Then he leaned over to Michael and whispered, " '*Till death do us part.*' I wish!"

As Ezra fumed, Megan asked, "So you're— you're all dead?"

"I'm afraid so," Emma said. "It's been one

hundred and twenty-two years since the black spell fell over this house. One hundred and twenty-two years since she died."

"Who?" Megan asked.

"Elizabeth," Emma said. "The woman from the portrait."

Megan turned back to the painting and stared at the woman's face. "She looks just like our mom," she said.

"Yes," said Emma. "Some people believe that they are one and the same."

"Please!" Ezra cried. "Enough! Are you being paid by the word?"

Megan was shocked. "Who was she?" she asked.

Emma lowered her head sadly. "She was the very heart of this house," she said. "She grew up here. She was . . . she was our friend. We loved her."

Groaning, Ezra rolled his eyes and slapped his forehead.

"Oh, you loved her, too, you insensitive toad!" Emma snapped.

Long ago, a great tragedy took place in Gracey Manor.

Years later, the ominous Gracey Manor
seems to be waiting for something to happen.

Sara Evers marvels at the luxurious
interior of the old house.

**Mr Gracey is a handsome, cultured gentleman –
but he seems to harbour a dark and heavy soul.**

The Evers family makes a stop at the old
mansion on their way to a weekend break.

Severe and proper, Ramsley, the butler,
runs Gracey Manor with an iron will.

Jim realizes that the mysteries of the
mansion run deeper than he thought.

Madame Leota, a spirit in a crystal ball, helps
Jim unearth Gracey Manor's chilling secrets.

Led by two helpful ghosts, Megan and Michael
find their own frights in the old house.

Jim and his kids get directions through the graveyard from a quartet of singing statues.

Jim and Megan find the key they need to unlock the final secret and save Sara Evers.

ZOMBIE ATTACK!

Jim fights to rescue his family
from a fate worse than death.

Ezra shrugged. "I respected her, certainly. She was an interesting conversationalist. She had a certain wit, yes. An unspoken charm . . ."

Ezra tried to hide his emotion as he wiped away a tear.

"But there's no reason to get sentimental!" he cried. "She's back! And now, now the curse will be broken! You see, it all works out in the end!"

"But what if it's not her?" Emma asked.

"It's not for us to question!" said Ezra. "The master knows best!"

Emma suddenly tensed with fear, as though she could hear something terrible the others could not.

"Hide!" she whispered anxiously to the children as she ushered them behind a stack of trunks.

Ramsley stepped from the shadows. "The children are not in their room," he said. "Have you seen them?"

"What children?" Emma asked innocently.

"The children *she* wasn't supposed to bring – along with that husband of hers," Ramsley said with a scowl. "If you find the children, bring them to me."

"Of course, sir," Emma and Ezra said in unison.

"Good," Ramsley said. He started to leave but then paused, as though he could sense something wasn't quite right. He shrugged off the sensation and added, "The final arrangements have been made. Nothing further will interfere with the master's plan."

Thunder rumbled and rain cascaded down the windows as Gracey led Sara into a glass atrium.

"This house was once filled with so many things," Gracey said. "So much life. Grand parties, dancing and laughter . . . and hope. Being a Gracey meant you were denied nothing. The world was yours."

A pained smile of regret crossed his lips.

"What happened here, Mr Gracey?" Sara asked.

"Elizabeth," said Gracey. "Hers is the story of

this house. The story that haunts these walls."

Jim ran up the stairs through the corridor, the eyes of the statues watching him as he passed. He was screaming at the top of his lungs. A ghostly combo of floating horns and tambourines now chased close on his heels, playing themselves loudly – and forcing Jim in the direction they wanted him to go.

Jim saw the attic door and charged through it. He slammed the door and scrambled to find the lock.

Megan and Michael turned at the commotion.

"Dad!" said Megan.

Jim turned and threw his back against the door as a barricade against the possessed musical instruments.

"Michael, Megan," he said, panting. "Get your things. We're leaving!"

He turned and locked the door, then ran to his kids and hugged them hard.

"Dad, we have a problem!" Megan said.

"I don't care about the rain," Jim said. "Let's get your mother and get outta here!"

"I'm afraid that's not possible," Ezra said.

For the first time Jim noticed the ghosts floating next to him. He put his arms around Megan and Michael and walked them quickly towards the stairs. "Come on, kids," he said. "Daddy's having more hallucinations."

"They're ghosts," Megan explained.

"They're not ghosts," Jim said. "It must have been the chicken. It didn't taste right. But we're still getting out of here!"

"Hey, it wasn't the chicken," Emma protested, defending her cooking.

"Okay. Not the chicken," Jim said. "We're still getting out of here."

"But, Dad," Megan said, resisting. "We have to help them!"

"See, if they are ghosts, they're already dead," explained Jim succinctly. "They're beyond help. That's the nature of being dead."

"The man's talking sense," Ezra put in with an

approving nod.

"But we have to help them break the curse!" Megan insisted.

"Why is everyone around here talking about a curse?" Jim asked, exasperated. "You! Her! The crazy green Gypsy in the giant paperweight!"

"Gypsy?" Emma said excitedly. "He found the Gypsy!"

Emma disappeared, then reappeared in front of Jim. "What did she say exactly?" Emma asked. "We have to go back to see her!"

"Go back?" Jim said. "No way!"

"But, Dad—" Megan said.

"Floating around a room upside down!" Jim said, still trying to lead his children away. "I lost my change—"

He stopped as he caught sight of the portrait of Elizabeth.

Michael and Megan said, "Mom's in trouble."

Jim stared at the portrait, stunned.

"What kind of trouble?"

Chapter 10

"She was of unsurpassed beauty," Gracey said. He walked around the atrium, staring at Sara. "More lovely than the heart could bear."

Feeling his gaze upon her, Sara turned, smiling. Gracey looked away.

"Her father was once the caretaker of this manor," Gracey continued. "But sadly, soon after she was brought into this world, he died, and the child was left alone with no kin to call her own. So, as a debt to her father, whom the family loved dearly, they took the girl in and raised her as one of their own. As an equal."

Gracey turned back to Sara, and in his mind's eye, beautiful amber rays of enchanted sunlight cascaded into the room all around her.

"This house was never so full of happiness as when she smiled," Gracey continued, and a spectral young boy joined a ghostly girl, laughing and chasing her around the room.

"And it was here, in this house, that the girl grew into a most beautiful young woman."

The girl was now a woman, laughing, running playfully.

"And it was here, in this house, she fell in love. Deeply, madly in love."

The young woman was caught from behind and spun around. The woman looked exactly like Sara. A younger Gracey kissed her. Their laughter echoed in Gracey's ears as he returned to the present. He looked at Sara. She was staring at him, lost in the ghostly images of his story, which seemed to come alive before her eyes.

"But it was a love that could not be," Gracey said, staring forlornly out of the window. "For she fell in love with the very heir to the house of Gracey. He had wealth, privilege, status and she was— she was not his kind. Those closest to the boy, who knew of his secret love, warned him of the tragedy that could befall."

Now Gracey bit his lower lip, obviously in emotional pain.

"But he loved her and would not be made to live a lie. So, foolishly, selfishly, he forced her to choose."

The two young ghosts became older. The young man was obviously Gracey. And the young woman looked just like Sara. The scene around them turned into a grand ball as Gracey continued his story.

"Run away from this place," Gracey said, recalling the choice he had asked the girl to make. "Run away from the world. Its rules, its prejudice. Run away and find a place in which they could love. Or, if not, never see him again. Her very presence would cause him too much pain."

Gracey turned back to Sara. "She told him she would give her reply the next evening, the night of the grand masquerade ball. She was to send him a letter . . ."

Now Gracey was hearing the distant echoes of a waltz from long ago. He saw the ghosts of guests appear, dancing around the room.

"She loved him so deeply, so dearly . . ."

Now Gracey saw a letter on white paper in a man's hands and heard a woman's voice reading the words contained in it:

"*. . . that I cannot, I should not be the reason for giving away your life, your world. But I cannot live without you. I'd rather die than be without you.*"

Gracey saw himself, the man in the black cloak and porcelain mask, running through the shadows of the hall. Each tolling of an infernal clock was the sound of doom.

"He rushed to stop her, but it was too late. He found her lying on the library floor."

Gracey saw himself carrying the woman's limp body, Elizabeth's body, through the corridors, the masked guests separating for him.

"He slipped deeper and deeper into the darkness. Possessed by the notion of bringing her back. Raising her from the very dead."

Gracey came back to the present. He was staring out at the storm.

"Obsessed with the black arts . . . ," he continued, "the ways of sorcery and dark magic. He tried to reach her, but he could not. It drove him to madness. And he cursed this mansion, cursing it until his one true love would at last return. Cursing it and all who would ever dare enter."

Sara stared at Gracey. She was overwhelmed. "That's . . . quite a story," she said.

"If you listen," Gracey said, "you can still hear the beat of her broken heart."

And indeed, at that moment, Sara was almost sure she could hear the sound of a distant heartbeat. But then she assured herself that it was just the thunder.

Meanwhile, in Madame Leota's room, Jim, the kids, and the ghosts had watched the entire scene as Gracey had described it to Sara in Madame Leota's crystal ball. As the image of Gracey faded, Madame Leota's visage returned.

Jim and the kids were stunned. "Okay, wait a second," Jim said. "Wait a second. Are you telling me he's dead? And we were brought here because he wants to get jiggy with my wife?"

"Pretty much," Ezra said. He eyed Jim, and then cast a knowing look at Emma. "Are you upset?"

Disgusted, Jim said, "Come on, kids. Let's get your mom and get out of here."

"You will fail," Madame Leota warned.

"Oh, Madame Leota," Emma said. "Is it her?"

"It is true," Madame Leota said. "She walks these halls."

Ezra rushed over to Emma. "Hah! You see? I told you! It *is* her!"

"But do not be deceived!" continued Madame Leota. "All things are not as they appear."

"Hah!" said Emma. "You see, it *isn't* her!"

"I'm so confused," Ezra moaned.

"For all secrets to be known," said Madame Leota, "you must find the key. The key that will unlock the truth."

"What key?" Jim exploded. "What truth?"

"The truth that will reveal all secrets—" Madame Leota said.

"What secrets?" said Jim. "What are you talking about? Secrets?"

"Hey!" barked Madame Leota. "*Listen!* I'm speaking in plain English! If you would shut up for just a second and let me get a word in edgewise, *maybe* I could tell you!"

There was a stunned silence as Madame Leota took a moment to regain her mystical composure. Then she continued.

"For your family to save, you must dig deep, deep into the grave. Enter the tomb under the great dead oak and travel down deep under the ground, and there you will find the key that must be found."

"Is somebody writing this down?" Jim asked out of the corner of his mouth.

"Find the black crypt that bears no name," said Madame Leota, "or soon your fate will be the same."

"Can you draw us a map or something?" Jim asked.

"The key must be found," Madame Leota screeched. "The key is the answer to all!"

"Great," Jim said. "Key answer to all. But how do we get outta here?"

"Well . . . " Ezra said thoughtfully. "There is always my way . . ."

Chapter 11

Jim, Megan and Michael found themselves crammed into a glass case in the back of an ethereal black hearse pulled by a ghostly mare. They flew through the mansion's walls and out into the graveyard. Jim and the kids were thrown about as the hearse hit every cobblestone and rock along the way.

In the driver's seat, Ezra wore a pair of old-fashioned goggles and held tight to the reins. Emma bounced and jostled next to him, holding on for dear afterlife.

"I thought you said you could drive this thing!" Jim cried from the back.

"Don't worry," Ezra shouted back with

umtamed glee. "I know what I'm doing."

"You do?" Emma asked as they hit another bump.

"Not exactly," Ezra told her with a devilish it's-too-late-to-stop-now grin.

"You're choking up on the reins," she cried.

"Do I tell you how to fluff up a pillow?" Ezra asked.

"No," said Emma. "Because I *know* how to fluff up a pillow. You're going to kill us all!"

"Ha, some of us are already dead!" Ezra replied.

Suddenly, a low branch came into view. Ezra and Emma screamed as the branch lopped off their heads in a shower of blue ghost dust.

Ezra's body continued to drive as he yanked hard on the reins. Both ghosts' heads re-formed as the hearse slowed.

"Whoa!" Ezra called. "Whoa, girl! Whoa!"

Jim, Megan and Michael were jostled again by the sudden change in speed. Jim muttered, "Man! Dead people have *no* consideration for the living."

Jim and the kids looked around in wonder. The graveyard was in full spectral swing! Ghosts and ghouls were flying all over the place, playing music, dancing, riding bikes, sipping tea . . . all in all, having a fabulously undead time.

"Who are these people?" Jim asked.

"Restless spirits," Emma told him. "When they died, they couldn't find the light to the other side and now they're trapped."

"Doomed to wander the earth," Ezra said sadly. And then, for effect, he added in an ominous voice, *"Doomed!"*

As Jim took in the bizarre party going on around him, he mumbled to himself, "The fabric of my reality is seriously unravelling."

Megan and Michael were also unable to believe what they were seeing.

"Kids, I think I let you down," Jim said. "I tried to prepare you for life, but I think I left a few things out."

"Like death?" Megan asked.

"Pretty much," Jim replied, and then they both chuckled as she rolled her eyes at him.

Finally, the hearse came to a stop. Jim thankfully opened the top of the glass case and tumbled over the side to the ground with a thud. He stood and shook off the effects of the ride and then helped Megan and Michael out of the hearse. The cemetery was quiet now. All the ghosts were gone.

"Well, thanks for the lift," Jim said to Ezra and Emma, still annoyed by the bumpy ride. "If we split up, we'll cover more ground."

"Good thinking," said Ezra. "We'll go this way."

The ghostly horse suddenly whinnied and the glass hearse took off into the night, Ezra and Emma still bickering about who should drive. Jim and the kids were left in the silent graveyard alone.

Back in the mansion, Sara slowly opened the lid of the intricately carved music box Gracey had handed her. A haunting melody emanated from the box as soon as the lid was opened completely.

"He made that for her," Gracey said.

"It's beautiful," Sara replied, admiring the craftsmanship.

"He did it to remind himself of happier times," Gracey told her sombrely. "Their last moments together."

"To love someone so much and lose them . . . " Sara said.

Gracey thought quietly for a moment and then a hopeful smile brightened his face.

"When you truly love someone, they never leave you. They remain in your heart forever."

Chapter 12

Everything was damp from the fog, and the ground was soft and muddy. Jim looked down at his expensive shoes as they sank into the mud.

"Man, these were my new Italian loafers," he said sadly.

"Well," said Megan. "Now they're your new Italian galoshes."

Jim ignored Megan's comment. He turned to Michael. "Was anybody paying attention?"

"I think the Gypsy lady said something about making a left at an oak tree," Michael said.

Jim looked around. There were oak trees everywhere. He said, "I'm glad she was so specific."

Megan thought for a moment. "She said, 'Find the tomb under the great dead oak.' "

As they turned to look again at the trees, they heard singing – the sound of a barbershop quartet. They followed the tune to four cemetery busts on pedestals singing in unison.

"All right, whatever," Jim said, accepting the situation. "Hey, do you guys know the way to the mausoleum?"

The busts replied in song:
"Down by the old mill stream,
By the light . . . by the light
Of the silvery moon . . ."

"Groovy, man. We'll buy the album," Jim interrupted. "I gotta help my wife—"

But the busts broke into another song, despite Jim's attempts to get them to help.

"Forget it," said Jim, irritated. He and the kids walked away, the quartet of ghosts still singing. A few minutes later, the moon came out from behind the clouds and shone down on a giant dead oak directly in front of them. Sitting in the oak's shadow was a round stone mausoleum.

They walked towards the mausoleum, Michael hiding behind his dad. He got the scary feeling that the oak was staring at them. Then lightning flashed, and they saw the name GRACEY etched into the arch of the mausoleum.

"Okay, we made it," Jim said. As he took a step closer, torches on both sides of the mausoleum's doors burst into flame.

Jim swallowed, then grabbed his kids' hands and stepped up to the iron doors.

"There's an inscription," Megan said.

Jim took one of the torches out of its bracket and held it up to get a better look.

"Latin," he said. "Why are things like this always in Latin? Nobody speaks Latin."

"Beware all who— all who enter," Megan said, slowly translating the inscription. "Here lies the passage . . . to the dead."

Jim was staring at his daughter in amazement. "Since when do you speak Latin?" he asked.

"I studied it for three years, Dad," Megan said. "You thought it was dumb, remember? You said it was a dead language."

Jim looked thoughtfully around the cemetery. "Yeah, well," he said dryly, "I guess I was wrong on that one. All right, let's get this key and—"

The mausoleum door moaned on its ancient hinges as it slowly opened.

Jim held the torch up. Inside the mausoleum they saw cobwebs everywhere. A spider skittered away from the light.

Michael stood frozen to the spot, staring at the cobwebs. He started to walk away.

"Come on, Michael," Jim said. "There's nothing to be afraid of."

Michael looked at his dad as if Jim had lost his mind. "I have to disagree."

"But this is no time to be scared," Jim said patiently. "You're a man now. You're ten, remember?"

"I just turned ten," Michael said. "I'm still getting used to it."

Jim looked at his son with concern, but he decided to drop the matter. He was scared, too, but he would do whatever he had to do for Sara and the kids. And right now, he had to find that key, and the mausoleum and whatever might be inside it were waiting.

"All right," Jim said. "Megan, stay with your brother."

"What?" Megan asked, shocked.

"You heard me," said Jim. "Stay with your brother. I'm not leaving him out here alone. Don't worry. I'll be right back."

"Twenty minutes tops, right?" said Megan.

"Right," said Jim. He looked into the dark tomb. "This is gonna be a piece of cake. Michael, watch your sister."

Then Jim, torch in hand, stepped into the tomb.

Chapter 13

Jim started to walk down the stone steps, pushing cobwebs out of his way. Near the bottom of the stairs, the room opened out into a vast circular tomb. Rainwater had collected on the floor, several feet deep. Coffins were stacked one on top of the other along the walls. Larger crypts were arranged across the floor of the room. They were submerged in rainwater up to their lids. Rats scurried everywhere.

"Mmm," Jim said. "What did the Gypsy say again? Look for a . . . look for a crib— crib? Did she say crypt? No, find . . . find—"

"The crypt with no name," said Megan. She was standing right behind Jim. He screamed.

"Megan, what are you doing down here?" Jim asked. "I thought I told you to stay with Michael."

"I was worried you wouldn't be able to find it," Megan said. "Michael's fine. She said, 'Find the black crypt that bears no name or soon your fate will be the same.' "

They scanned the room. On a circular platform in the centre of the mausoleum sat a large black crypt. Moonlight shone down on it from the dome overhead.

"Okay," Jim said. "That might be it."

"Good hunch," Megan said dryly. "Come on."

To the side of the stairs was a crumbling stone bridge that led over the water to the platform. With Megan leading the way, they started to walk across.

"Man, I am so officially sick of this place," Jim said.

"And we're here because of whom?" Megan asked. Jim was shocked and a little hurt. So Megan quickly added, "Come on, let's get this over with."

She reached down and lifted the stone lid. It creaked open. In the crypt lay a decomposed body in a tattered suit. One of the corpse's hands clutched a large key.

"It's the key!" Megan said. She reached in and grabbed it. "Well, that wasn't so hard? Was it?"

As Jim took the key from his daughter, the rats all around them started squeaking in panic. Jim and Megan watched them flee the platform, skittering across the bridge and up the stairs.

"Huh," said Jim. "Must be dinner-time."

Behind him, Jim heard an odd wheezing. He turned and found himself face to face with the corpse from the crypt! It was sitting up and looking right at him.

Jim screamed, accidentally tossing the key into the air. It skipped across the platform and dropped into the water.

"Dad!" Megan cried in horror.

"Get the key!" Jim called, watching the zombie slowly rise from its coffin. "Get the key! I'll take care of this!"

Megan jumped off the platform into the dirty

water. Bones floated up all around her as she started feeling around for the key.

Jim circled the zombie, bobbing and weaving and shuffling his feet.

"Oh, you're not too fast, are you, dead man?" Jim taunted. He swung his torch at the dead thing and the zombie's head popped clean off.

"Yeah!" Jim cried. "How you like me now? You're gonna think twice before you come back from the dead again, aren't ya, dead man?"

Jim turned to Megan. "Did you get the key?" he asked.

"I'm looking! I'm looking!" Megan cried.

"All right, well, take your time," Jim said. "I've got everything under . . ."

Jim was momentarily speechless as he noticed the lids of all the crypts on the floor of the tomb beginning to slide. The bodies inside all of them had come to life.

"Okay, look faster!" Jim called.

"Do you want to get down here and help?" Megan asked in frustration.

Lids slid off crypts, and zombies began to rise

all around them.

"I think I just got a little busy up here!" Jim said as more reanimated corpses opened their crypts and caskets.

Megan shook her head. This wasn't working. She couldn't find the key. She was going to have to try something else.

"Oh, I don't want to do this—" she moaned. But she had no choice. Taking a deep breath, she ducked under the water.

It was strangely quiet. Then she noticed skeletons swimming towards her. She pawed through the muck on the floor until she saw the key. She grabbed it and shot back to the surface.

"Got it!" she shouted.

She heard a horrible moan, and a zombie leapt on her from behind! Megan screamed and swung round, trying to get him off, but it was no good, until—

"Hey!" Jim called.

The zombie turned to look at Jim. Using his torch as a bat, Jim swatted the zombie's head. The head fell to the ground.

Jim pointed at what was left of the zombie and angrily said, "*Don't* touch my daughter." He grabbed Megan's hand. "Come on, let's—" Jim broke off as they turned and found a wall of zombies slowly moving towards them.

"Let's not panic. Let's not panic," Jim said. He and Megan backed up the stairs of the central platform and discovered that the zombies had completely surrounded it. They climbed up onto the black crypt.

"Okay, now we can panic," Jim said.

But Megan had an idea. "Dad— swing me!"

"What?" Jim asked.

"Do you remember when we were kids, and you used to swing me?" she asked.

"Megan, this is no time for fun and games!" Jim scolded.

"Dad!" Megan said. "Trust me. Do it!"

It took a second, but then Jim understood what she was getting at. Grabbing Megan by the forearms, he started spinning in a circle. Megan's legs lifted off the ground and smashed into the zombies. The zombies knocked into each other and fell like dominoes.

Jim lowered Megan to the platform and leapt down from the crypt to join her. "Nice call," he said.

"Thanks," Megan said.

They splashed through the water towards the steps. All around them, more crypts opened. Zombies reached out to grab them as they passed. Megan and Jim jumped out of the water onto the steps and hurried up towards the mausoleum doors.

Ahead they could see the door. It was open, and Michael stood outside it, quivering with fear.

"It's okay, Michael," Jim said. "We're coming! We're—"

They watched in horror as the mausoleum door slowly started to swing closed. Just as Jim and Megan got to it, the door slammed shut!

Chapter 14

Jim threw his shoulder against the iron door and tried to open it.

"Great," he said. "Locked from the outside. Michael! Michael, open the door!"

But Michael was frozen with terror. The outside of the door was covered with spiders – really big spiders.

"Michael, can you hear me?" Jim called. "Open the door!"

But Michael couldn't take his eyes off the huge spiders climbing all over the door. "I can't!" he said.

"What do you mean, you can't?" Jim said. "Just open the door!"

Behind them Jim and Megan heard the zombies moaning.

"There are spiders everywhere!" Michael called back.

Jim looked down and saw some large spiders scurrying under the door of the tomb. He looked back over his shoulder. There were zombie-like shadows at the bottom of the stairs. Megan tugged on her dad's shirt. "They're coming!"

Jim turned back to the door. "Michael, I know that you're scared. Everyone gets scared, but you can't let that stop you."

"If you think you're scared now," Megan interjected, "wait until the zombies come out!"

"Would you just stop it," Jim hissed at Megan. Turning back to the door, he said as calmly as possible, "Please, Michael. We're running out of time."

Michael took a step closer to the door. The spiders were big. They were crawling all over each other and the door.

Taking a deep breath, Michael closed his eyes. Determined, he reached out and stuck his hand into the spiders. Immediately, they started swarming up his arm. He whimpered as he felt around for the lock.

On the other side of the door, the zombies were now shuffling up the stairs.

"Dad!" Megan yelled, glancing nervously over her shoulder. "They're coming!"

Michael was sure he couldn't take much more, but then he suddenly felt the lock. He pressed it. The lock clicked, and the doors sprang open. Jim and Megan tumbled out. Jim turned and slammed the door shut on the zombies.

Jim turned back and helped Michael flick off the remaining spiders. Then he hugged Michael hard.

"Are you okay?" Jim said. "Oh, my brave little man."

Megan hugged her little brother as well.

Michael looked his dad steadily in the eye and asked, "Did you get the key?"

Jim smiled at his son, proud of him. Then he held up the skeleton key.

Chapter 15

A little later, they were all back in Madame Leota's room. Jim held up the key.

"Okay, here, it is!" he said. "Now, where's the door to get us outta here?"

"First," said Madame Leota from her crystal ball, "you must find the trunk!"

"No door?" Jim stared at her. He couldn't believe it. "Trunk? Trunk! What are you talking about? You never said anything about any trunk!"

"No door," said Madame Leota. "You must open the trunk to find the truth!"

Jim looked at his kids and the ghosts, utterly flabbergasted. "All you said was get the key! I got the key, and now you're telling me a story about a trunk. The key is the answer to all, *remember?*"

"Look, I don't make the rules, okay?" Leota said. "I just work here."

"All right, that's it!" Jim said. He was fed up. He reached across the table and grabbed Leota's crystal ball. He hefted the ball in his hand. Jim was finally taking charge of the situation.

"What are you doing?" said Leota. "Put me down! This is bad luck! This is very bad luck!"

"Oh, I'll show you bad luck!" Jim said, bringing the ball close to his face so that Madame Leota could see he meant business. "I'm not playing with you any more!"

Upstairs, Ramsley opened the double doors to the ballroom, and Gracey and Sara walked through. The room was dimly lit by flickering candlelight. Portraits hanging on the wall stared down at them.

Ramsley smiled at Gracey as he closed the double doors, leaving them alone. Sara was gazing at a portrait of Gracey.

"And this," Gracey said, "this is where the story ends. This house has been waiting for so long to be lifted from its shroud of darkness. And tonight, for the first time, I believe that it may be possible for the story to end differently."

"Here?" Sara asked. "Why here?"

Gracey grimaced with pain at the memory of his dearly departed Elizabeth. Then he stared hopefully at Sara, the moonlight streaming down on them through the windows.

"Sara . . . do you believe that love is about second chances?" he asked. "About forgiveness?"

Sara stared at him for a moment, taking in his words. "Yes, I do," she said. "Mr Gracey, are you all right?"

Gracey had closed his eyes. "Do you not remember?" he asked.

"Remember what?" Sara asked.

"Do you not recognize me at all?" Gracey asked, becoming frustrated.

Sara smiled at him, a little confused. "From where, Mr Gracey?" she asked.

"I thought certainly bringing you here – to

Gracey Manor – would help you remember."

"What are you talking about?" Sara asked. "You're scaring me."

"This is where it happened," said Gracey, trying to jog Sara's memory. "Where we spent our last moments together. Where we danced for one last time. I held you so tight in my arms. I thought we would be together forever. And now you have returned to me!"

Sara stepped away from Gracey, suddenly wary.

Tears streamed down Gracey's face. "Why do you not remember? You were my world! My life! And I have loved you in death as I have in life!"

Sara turned and ran out of the room – but Gracey was somehow there, walking towards her.

"The sun has died a thousand times, but I have never stopped loving you!" he said. "And now, after an eternity, we can be together."

Shaking with fear, Sara turned and ran up the stairs. Gracey was there, walking down the stairs towards her.

"You are she!" Gracey said. He was clearly

becoming distraught. "You are Elizabeth! You must be!"

Sara pushed past Gracey. She cried out for her husband.

"Search your heart!" Gracey called. "I am your one love! And now— we will be together. There is nothing stopping us now."

Sara ran down the corridor. Gracey materialized in front of her once more. Sara dived into her bedroom and locked the door.

"She does not remember," he said. "It cannot be she."

Ramsley was standing beside him. "It is she, sir," he said. "The Gypsy woman prophesied her return."

Ramsley looked at Gracey with fatherly concern and straightened Gracey's tie.

"You had better get ready," Ramsley said. "The hour approaches."

"But she does not remember," Gracey said.

"In time she will, sir," Ramsley replied. "I assure you."

Chapter 16

The attic was dark and quiet. A floorboard creaked and began to rise. An eerie greenish light illuminated the room as Jim used Madame Leota's ball like a flashlight. He, the kids and the ghosts, Ezra and Emma, searched for the trunk.

Annoyed, Madame Leota peered around the room. "Careful! I'm fragile!"

"Hey, don't talk to me about fragile," Jim said, climbing the rest of the way into the attic. "I'm the one feeling fragile!"

"Oh, this is getting exciting!" Ezra said.

Emma glanced around the attic fearfully. "We shouldn't be here," she said. "What if we get caught?"

"Oh, now look who's in a fearful dither," Ezra said, teasing his wife.

Jim spotted a large black trunk with golden moulding. "Is that it?" he asked Madame Leota.

"That's it," she said, squinting in the darkness.

Jim knelt down in front of the trunk. He licked his lips as he tried the key in the old lock. It clicked open.

He swallowed nervously, then raised the lid. Inside the trunk he saw some neatly folded clothes. On top of the clothes rested a letter in a red envelope. He carefully lifted it out of the trunk. He turned it over. It was addressed to "My Love".

Jim opened the letter and began to read:

"*Yes. My dear heart, I will be with you. I will love you for all eternity. And tonight, at last, we will be together. I do!*"

Out of the corner of his eye, Michael caught sight of flickering candlelight. He froze with fear.

Emma stared at Jim in shock and exclaimed, "She didn't kill herself!"

"She wanted to be with him," Ezra said. Then

the ghosts saw what Michael had seen in the shadows and they also froze.

"Somebody gave him the wrong letter," Jim said as everything came together in his mind.

From behind him Ramsley said, "Yes. Well done, Mr Evers."

Ramsley was dressed in a black formal coat that somehow made him look that much more stiff and impersonal. Michael and Megan inched closer to Jim.

"I must say I am impressed," Ramsley continued. "You're more persistent than I would have ever imagined."

Ramsley turned to Ezra and Emma, his stare cold and hard. "I'll deal with you two later."

"The butler did it!" Jim exclaimed. "You have got to be kidding me. Why did you do it?"

Ramsley tidied up a pile of clothes, stacking them neatly. "The master would not listen to reason. He had everything in the world and yet he was willing to throw it all away for love. I did tell her it would end badly."

"You are one cold man," Jim said.

"I am a rational man, Mr Evers," Ramsley said coolly. "It was my responsibility to the house, and my duty to see to it that the boy didn't make a foolish error in judgment. Running away with that girl would have destroyed this house. And, of course, I simply could not stand by and see that happen."

As Ramsley told his story, a spectral version of it played before everyone's eyes:

A younger Ramsley whispers in Gracey's ear. Gracey excuses himself, leaving the butler alone with his beloved.

Ramsley pours a drink for Elizabeth and congratulates her.

"You approve?" she asks, thinking that of all people, the stiff and proper butler would be the first to object to her union with Gracey.

"Of course," says Ramsley, handing her the goblet of wine. "I want nothing but the master's happiness. So let us drink to the future."

Elizabeth takes the goblet of wine and accepts Ramsley's toast. A smile crosses her face, and then she takes a drink. Suddenly, her smile fades. Stricken, she collapses to the floor next to a roaring fireplace.

"So you killed her," Jim said.

"Punch his face in," Megan urged.

"First, I am gonna tell his master what really happened," Jim said, staring Ramsley straight in the eye.

"I'm afraid that is out of the question," said Ramsley. "The master must never know. The only thing that matters now is that this curse be broken."

"Well, you caused it!" Jim said.

"Yes," Ramsley agreed. "But now I'm going to end it. Edward and his love will be reunited. And we can all move on. Yes, this house *will* once again be clean."

"But that's not her!" Jim protested, thinking of Sara. "That's my wife."

"This is of little importance," Ramsley said. "The master's pain must end, Mr Evers."

Jim stared angrily at Ramsley. "Where's my wife?" he asked.

"Why, she's getting ready for her wedding, of course," Ramsley replied.

"He can't marry her!" Jim exclaimed. "She's married! *And* she's not dead!"

"True," said Ramsley. "But that can be easily corrected. Life, I'm afraid, is such a delicate state."

Angrily, Jim rushed at Ramsley, but he passed right through the ghostly butler!

Ramsley laughed with sinister glee.

"Listen to me!" Jim said. "You are going to get Sara, and you are going to let us out of here! Do you hear me?"

"You want out?" Ramsley said. "Fine."

The butler's hand solidified, and he grabbed Jim by the throat. Ramsley lifted him off the ground and floated over to an open window.

"Now, for the last time, goodnight, Mr Evers," Ramsley said, mocking his own formal tone. With an evil grin, Ramsley thrust Jim over the edge of the window and let him go.

Megan and Michael screamed. But their screams were cut short by a large black trunk that swept up behind them and snapped tightly around them. They were trapped.

Jim fell helplessly, finally smacking into the

glass roof of the conservatory. He slid painfully down the glass and fell onto the hood of his car, setting off its screeching alarm. Then he rolled onto the muddy ground.

Jim looked at the mansion. All the shutters and doors slammed closed. Lightning flashed and thunder roared as all the locks clicked shut. Jim was banished from Gracey Manor for good.

He got up and grabbed a long piece of discarded wrought-iron fence. He began to furiously smash it against the house, but it barely scratched the ancient masonry.

His car alarm still blaring, Jim turned on his prized possession and began to smash the hood, the rear-view mirrors, the windshield and anything else that would break. Finally, exhausted, he dropped to the ground.

"Shut up!" he groaned at the ruined car. The alarm continued to whine for a moment and then it faded out. For the first time in his life, Jim Evers felt totally defeated.

Back in the bedroom, Sara was searching for a way out – but all the doors and windows were sealed. Suddenly, she felt a chill. She knew she wasn't alone and so she spun around. Ramsley stood behind her.

"There's something horribly wrong," Sara said, running to the butler for help. "Mr Gracey . . . he's . . ."

"I know, dear," Ramsley said soothingly. "He's expecting you. You can't keep the master waiting."

"For what?" Sara asked.

"Your wedding."

Ramsley smiled as Sara backed away from him, horrified. She glanced at the bed. A wedding dress was laid out there.

"I'm not Elizabeth!" she protested.

Ramsley smiled. "But of course you are, my dear," he said. "Put on your dress."

"You don't think I'm going through with this madness, do you?" Sara said defiantly.

"I very much do," Ramsley said. "You see . . ."

Ramsley raised his eyes and looked over Sara's shoulder. She turned to see Michael and Megan appear in the mirror above the night table. They had been shoved into a black trunk and were helpless. Two armoured knights held axes over their heads.

"We wouldn't want anything to happen to the children, now, would we?" Ramsley asked.

Sara stared helplessly.

"The master believes you are his one true Elizabeth," Ramsley said. "Therefore, it must be so. If not . . . hmm . . . I really do fear for the children."

Sara turned back to the mirror, crying. Ramsley reached out and caressed her hair. "Oh, you will make such a lovely bride," he said, his smile thin and cruel.

He left the room. Out in the corridor, Ezra and Emma stood at attention.

"Have her ready," Ramsley said to the ghosts. "And this time . . ."

He drew close to them. ". . . any further acts of insubordination will be dealt with in the harshest possible manner."

"But, sir," Emma protested.

"There are worse things than purgatory,"

Ramsley added, coming nose to nose with her.
"I can assure you."

Chapter 17

In the grand hallway the grandfather clock began to strike the hour. The twelve at the top of the dial slowly changed into a thirteen.

Outside the mansion, Jim sat in the mud, his head down. He listened to the clock chiming. As the last chime faded, he lifted his head and stared at the house looming above him.

From his right a voice asked, "What are you doing?"

Jim glanced over. It was Madame Leota, her crystal ball half buried in the mud. Jim groaned, "Just leave me alone."

"I made us come here," he suddenly confessed. "We should have been at the lake. And now it's too late. I've lost them."

"It's never too late, Mr Evers," Madame Leota said.

"I can't get back in. I tried," Jim complained in defeat. "What do you want me to do?"

Madame Leota stared at him for a moment and then said simply, "Try again."

In the ballroom Ezra sat at the pipe organ and played a hideously macabre version of the wedding march. Gracey waited excitedly at the end of the aisle. Acting as bridesmaid, Emma stood across the aisle. Ramsley stood above them all, presiding.

Ezra paused in his playing, and the room's double doors swung open. Sara stood behind them, dressed in the wedding gown. Ezra began playing "Here Comes the Bride" as Sara walked down the aisle.

Emma and Ezra looked down in shame as Sara reached them at the altar. Gracey looked deep into her eyes.

"Elizabeth?" he asked.

"Yes . . . my love," she said tearfully.

Ramsley smiled down wickedly from the altar.

Meanwhile, outside the mansion, Jim was sitting in his ruined car and revving the engine. He turned to the passenger seat.

"Hang on," he said. In the passenger seat Leota's ball sat buckled in.

Jim punched the gas pedal, and the car rocketed forwards – right through the glass wall of the atrium. The car smashed into a grand piano, ploughing it across the room. Glass and dead flowers fell onto the car as Jim shouldered open his door.

"Stay there," Jim said to Leota. "I'll be right back."

"*Oh-keh*," Leota replied, her voice muffled by the passenger-side air bag.

Jim stormed into the armoury, following the sound of the organ. He rushed towards the doors of the ballroom, then stopped in his tracks. Two knights stood guard over Michael and Megan. The other suits of armour that lined the hall came to life, creaking as they turned their metal heads to face him.

"Dad!" the children both screamed.

There was a groan of rusty metal as the knights lifted their weapons in unison. Angered, Jim dived through the gauntlet of ancient knights. Two knights swung their swords at him. Jim ducked. Each knight's sword shattered the other, the empty armour falling to the ground in a heap.

Jim rolled away and got up as another knight stepped forwards, swinging a huge battle mace. This time, Jim jumped. The mace missed him and beheaded the next two knights in the line of death.

Jim dived through the legs of the mace-wielding knight – only to be confronted by yet another knight with a halberd, a combined battleaxe and spear. Jim dodged a killing blow – and then grabbed hold of the halberd. The knight lifted him into the air and tried to shake him off.

As Jim dangled over the floor, he saw the knight with the mace coming in for another blow. Jim let go of the axe just as the mace shattered its owner. Jim grabbed the halberd, swung with all his might and destroyed the mace-wielding knight.

He hopped up. Only two knights were left between Jim and his children. He had the hang of this battle thing. As the two knights approached him, he smiled and pulled the rug out from under them. The armour clattered to the floor.

"Kids, are you all right?" Jim asked Megan and Michael as he freed them from the trunk.

"Dad! We have to get Mom!" Megan cried, knowing there was not a second to lose.

Inside the ballroom Ramsley was conducting the wedding ceremony.

"And do you, Elizabeth Henshaw, take this man to be your lawful husband, to have and to hold, to love and cherish in death as in life?"

"I do," she said, trying to hold back a sob.

Ramsley made her drink from a goblet.

"What God has joined together, let no man cast asunder," Ramsley continued. "From this day forwards you will be joined together as one for all eternity. If anyone has any objections, let them—"

The ballroom doors crashed open. It was Jim! Sara recognized his determined look and breathed a sigh of relief.

"Yeah, I got a few objections!" Jim declared. Then he grabbed Sara and held her tight.

"I love you," she said, looking into his eyes.

"Next time I say we're going to the lake," Jim said, and this time he meant it, "we're going to the lake."

Gracey ran forwards, furious. "Get away from her!" he shouted. "I lost her once. I do not intend to let it happen again."

Jim pushed him away. "This isn't Elizabeth."

Gracey pulled out his sword. "I am warning you, sir. Step away from her."

"Go ahead, use it," Jim said, stepping in front of Sara and reaching for the red envelope in his pocket. "But before you do, you might want to read this."

Gracey took the letter and began reading.

"It's Elizabeth's letter. Her *real* letter," Jim told him. "The one Ramsley stole. The one you never saw."

Megan and Michael came running in behind him.

"What is the meaning of this?" Gracey asked Ramsley, shaking the letter in his hand. "It is written in her hand."

"Must we continue to listen to the ramblings of this lunatic?" Ramsley responded dryly, trying to calm his master.

"Well?" Gracey demanded.

Ramsley stared his master in the eye. When he realized that Gracey was not going to back down, the butler gave one of his cuffs a little tug, straightened his collar, and said, "Your union was unacceptable."

"So you killed her!" Gracey screamed.

"I told you it would be a mistake to run away with that girl," Ramsley said matter-of-factly.

"But I loved her," Gracey said feebly.

"You *ungrateful* fool!" Ramsley fumed. "All these years, I have sacrificed for you. But what would you understand about sacrifice, duty or honour?"

Ramsley's eyes lit up with demonic fury, and a maelstrom of wind raged around him, sending vases and statues crashing to the floor, knocking books from the shelves and blowing out the candles.

"You loved her? Damn you. Damn you to *hell*!"

Jim faced Ramsley in the onslaught, screaming, "Who do you think you are, damning us to hell? We didn't judge anybody. And we certainly didn't kill anybody. So as far as I am concerned, the only person around here going to hell is *you*!"

At his words the flames in the giant stone fireplace grew higher. Demons leapt from the flames and flew around the room. They grabbed Ramsley and started to drag him towards the burning hellfire.

As the demons shrieked in triumph of their

prize, Ramsley reached out and grabbed Jim's ankle. With nothing to hold on to, Jim was pulled towards the fire along with the condemned butler.

Suddenly, a hand reached out and grasped Jim's forearm. It was Gracey! With a frantic pull, he yanked Jim free of Ramsley and the demons.

The flames lashed out at the screaming butler, sucking him towards the abyss. The demons began to strip Ramsley's flesh from his bones as they fell into the flames, tumbling south of heaven. For a moment the fire blazed even more brightly, and the piteous howls of the damned filled the room. Then, with a mighty *whoosh*, Ramsley, the demons and the flames were gone.

Suddenly, Megan screamed. Her mother lay motionless on the floor.

Jim ran over to Sara. He knelt down and held Sara in his arms. The kids, the ghosts and Gracey stared down sadly.

"It's the poison," said Ezra.

"Sara, don't do this," Jim pleaded, tears welling up in his eyes. "Please. I love you so much."

From out of nowhere, they all heard a heartbeat coming from behind them. They turned and saw the ball of white light float into the room. It drifted down the aisle and settled into Sara's body. Sara rose off the floor and floated over the others. A shaft of heavenly light illuminated her. Her eyes opened. She looked down at everyone, then floated over to Gracey.

"Elizabeth?" Gracey asked. "Is it you?"

"Yes, my love," said the spirit of Elizabeth. She reached down and touched Gracey's face gently. "The truth had to be known for me to be released."

"I have waited so long . . . " Gracey sobbed.

"And now . . . only heaven awaits," Elizabeth said, kissing him.

Suddenly, there was a blast of brilliant light. Sara dropped into Jim's arms. She was blinking groggily.

"Jim?" she asked, dazed.

Jim squeezed her tightly. "Oh, Sara. I thought I lost you."

"And I thought I lost you," Sara whispered. She leaned up and kissed her husband.

"I hope you can forgive me," Gracey said to Jim, handing him a piece of paper. "Here. Take this. Thank you."

And with that, he walked back to the shaft of light and his waiting Elizabeth. His body also became light. The two lovers who had waited so long were together at last.

Jim looked down to see what Gracey had given him. It was the deed to the property. Jim was now the master of Gracey Manor.

Jim smiled and tossed the deed aside. He was going to need both hands free to give his family the biggest hug of their lives.

The curse was broken. Outside, all the ghosts were set free, their spirits rising towards a heavenly light.

Emma dragged two heavy bags with her. Ezra was flabbergasted.

"You can't take it with you," he said.

"The heck I can't," she replied, tossing him one of her bags to carry.

"Till death do us part," Ezra muttered as he entered the column of light. "I wish."

Epilogue

"Love endures all, no reason, no rhyme; it lasts forever, all the time," Madame Leota intoned, a faraway look in her eyes. Love had conquered all, and everything was as it should be.

"Won't you please shut up?" Megan said, exasperated with the newest addition to the Evers family.

"Are we there?" Michael asked, taking a big bite out of a chocolate bar.

"Yeah, I'm getting hungry, too," Megan added.

"Can we get pizza?" Michael shouted through a mouthful of chocolate.

Sara looked over at Jim and smiled. It was good to have the family back together again, safe and sound. Everyone was packed into the family's new van, which was crammed from top to bottom with bags, bicycles, camping gear and everything else the Everses would need for a much-deserved and long-overdue holiday.

"What do you think?" Jim asked Sara from the passenger seat. "How much longer?"

"Don't worry," Sara said. "Twenty minutes tops."

"That's crazy," Jim said, wishing he was driving. "Nothing takes twenty minutes."

"Well, you'd better hurry," Madame Leota chirped from the backseat, "because I've got to tinkle."

"Well, you should have thought of that before we left," Jim scolded.

"Hey, I can't predict everything," Madame Leota responded indignantly.

Jim chuckled. It was just like old times. The Evers family was happy.